Samantha
VanAlstyne

Tessa Rose
Hermance

Hi,
I'm Sam

To my nieces and nephews, Thank you for being the inspiration behind this book
-Auntie Sam

Hi, I'm Sam. Well actually my name is Samantha but I just like Sam. My favorite colors are pink, and purple and I was born on October 14th

My favorite holiday is Christmas and I really like chicken nuggets. I also have two brothers Will and Randy

I'm not exactly like Will and Randy though. They can walk and I use a wheelchair. I was born with cerebral palsy.

That's a scary sounding word for a not so scary thing. Cerebral palsy has a nickname, CP. That's a much easier thing to say.

Cerebral Palsy

When I was born I was born way too soon. My birthday is in October but the doctors had planned for me in January. That's three months too soon

Why I was born so early you might ask? The part of my mommy that was keeping me breathing separated from inside her. The doctors had to move fast

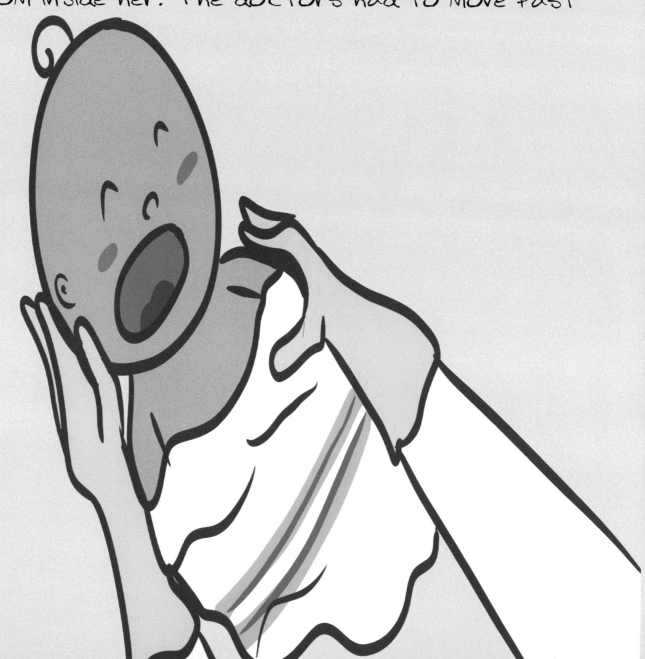

I weighed two pounds when I was born. That's as much as a pineapple or a pair of shoes. Teddy bears were bigger than me

I had to stay in the hospital a little while until I grew bigger. But, I made it home in time for my first Christmas.

Having a big brother helped my mom and dad realize that I was a little different. I didn't do things like other babies so to the doctor we went

It would be the first of hundreds
of doctor appointments in my life.
The doctor figured out that I
have CP using some kind of tests

The parts of my brain that help my legs move got damaged because I couldn't breathe. I can't walk like everyone else so I use a wheelchair

Vroom Vroom!

After a bunch of doctors said I could I finally got to go to school with all the other kids. I was so excited to ride the school bus. I was so tiny that I had to ride in a carseat on the bus.

WHEE!

On the first day of school I met Janet. My mom had picked Janet out especially to take care of me at school. Most of my classmates thought she was my mom.

I also made my very first friend. His name is Eddie and we're still friends as adults but in kindergarten he was just a nice kid with big ears

That was also the year I got my first official wheelchair. Before that I mostly used a stroller and went wherever someone put me

COOL!

My mom wasn't that interested in getting me a wheelchair at first. She was content to keep me in my stroller as long as possible

It wasn't until my mom's sister my Aunt Laurie introduced me to her friend Eddie that things changed.

Aunt Laurie's friend Eddie was also in a wheelchair. He was the first person in a wheelchair I'd ever met.

He explained to my mom the importance of having my own wheelchair. Eddie stressed that my mom wouldn't like it if someone left her in a corner and only moved her when they felt like it. So why would she want that for me?

Thankfully, my mom agreed and star
ed the process to get me a cha
When asked where he and my Aunt we
off to for the evening Eddie grinne
and replied "We're going dancin

I'M AMAZING!

That moment was magical for me. As a young girl who had never met anyone else like me. It showed me that I shouldn't let being a little different slow me down

As my mom has instilled in me for a·
long as I can remember can't isn'·
a word and all things are possible

So hi, my name is Sam and I have cerebral palsy. And that is totally okay. I wouldn't want to be anyone but me.

Acknowledgements

First I'd like to thank my illustrator Tessa for bringing my story to life. And a huge thank you to everyone who has supported me on this adventure.

CPSIA information can be obtained
at www.ICGtesting.com
Printed in the USA
LVHW070231250121
677402LV00018B/705